AL

For four kittens who taught me how to purr
and for Thérèse and Nanook
—G. M.

For my godmother and my grandparents
—X. D.

Copyright © 2006 by NordSüd Verlag AG, Gossau Zürich, Switzerland
First published in France under the title *Le temps des ronrons*
English translation copyright © 2006 by North-South Books Inc., New York.

First published in the United States, Great Britain, Canada, Australia, and New Zealand in 2006
by North-South Books, an imprint of NordSüd Verlag AG, Gossau Zürich, Switzerland.
Distributed in the United States by North-South Books Inc., New York.

Library of Congress Cataloging-in-Publication Data is available.
A CIP catalogue record for this book is available from The British Library.

ISBN-13: 978-0-7358-2062-3
ISBN-10: 0-7358-2062-7
1 3 5 7 9 10 8 6 4 2
Printed in Belgium

GÉRARD MONCOMBLE

Pippin

ILLUSTRATED BY XAVIÈRE DEVOS

Translated by Alexandra Simon

North-South Books

New York / London

Like all kittens, Pippin had soft fur, full whiskers, and knew how to use his claws. He was fantastic at meowing. But he was slow! So, so slow! That's what mother said. She had so much to do, she was always hurrying and running around. The days were just too short for everything she had to do.

"Hurry, Pippin," she'd say, trying to rush him along.

Pippin called his mother HurryMama. In secret, of course.

Pippin's father always got home from work very late. Often it was too late to give Pippin a good night hug because Pippin was already asleep. And in the morning, Pippin's father washed, dressed, and ate at top speed. He was never late for work. He was the most serious father in the world.

"Papa, could you . . ." Pippin would start to say.

"Later, Pippin," his father would cut him off.

Pippin called his father LaterPapa. In secret, of course.

HurryMama and LaterPapa loved their kitten very much. In fact, every Sunday they did special things with him. They'd take Pippin to the museum or to the movies. They'd go for rides in the car or in a boat. They'd visit famous buildings or go to the zoo.

"Hurry, Pippin!" said HurryMama when he'd start to dawdle. When Pippin wanted to sit down and take a break, LaterPapa would complain, "Later, son."

Pippin's head spun round and round like a merry-go-round. Sundays were like whirlwinds!

Even though HurryMama and LaterPapa were very, very busy, there was something they'd noticed and it bothered them. Pippin didn't purr. He meowed plenty, but he didn't purr.

HurryMama and LaterPapa were baffled. All cats purr. Every single one! Why not Pippin?

As far as HurryMama was concerned, Pippin couldn't learn to purr fast enough. She wanted him purring immediately! LaterPapa calmed her down, "Don't worry! He'll learn sooner or later!"

But the weeks passed, the Sundays whirled around, and Pippin still didn't purr.

At last Pippin's parents decided to consult a doctor.

Doctor Dog got out his stethoscope and listened to Pippin's chest. "Hmmm," muttered Doctor Dog, "if he doesn't start purring soon we may have to operate!" Pippin panicked. An operation? He didn't even know what that was, but he knew he didn't want one. There was only one thing to do. He'd have to learn how to purr. And he knew he'd never learn at home, where everything either moved too fast or was put off until later.

So Pippin decided to find someone who could teach him how to purr.

Pippin wandered around, not knowing where he was going. Suddenly, he heard an enormous purring sound coming from their neighbor Mr. Bear's house.

That's what I need, he thought, a purring teacher.

Pippin went into the house. There he found Mr. Bear asleep in a chair, snoring ten times louder than LaterPapa snored. Pippin listened carefully. With each purr, the house shook from the floor to the ceiling. Pippin tapped on the bear's belly, and Mr. Bear opened an eye.

"I would like to learn to purr," said Pippin.

"Get out! I'm sleeping!" yelled Mr. Bear in a horrible voice that shook the walls, the sidewalks, and even the pavement in the street outside.

Pippin left quickly. Anybody that grumpy wouldn't be a good purring teacher anyway.

A bit farther along the street, Pippin heard sputtering, and then a roar. It sounded like a purring concert! Pippin decided to go into the garage and ask for a lesson.

"I would like to learn how to purr," he said to the mechanic. But only the motor answered, *Putt, putt, pppppuuuuut*, and covered Pippin with a thick cloud of smelly, black smoke.

"Rats," grumbled the mechanic, who was lying under the car. "What do I have to do to get you to run, you blasted tank on wheels!"

Pippin learned some new words—but not how to purr.

Pippin did not give up. He walked on and, suddenly, he heard a noise coming from a tree. Was it the rustling of the leaves or the sound of the wind? Without another thought, he bounded up the tree. But it was the buzzing of bees in the tree. They were searching for pollen, and they didn't like being bothered. They attacked poor Pippin, who ran back down the tree as fast as he could. Luckily he escaped the bees' stingers. Unfortunately, he also escaped another possible purring lesson.

Almost any other kitten would have given up by now. But not Pippin. He was determined.

He listened to the hum of a fan, the rat-a-tat-tat of a jackhammer, the roar of an airplane, and the clip-clip-clip of a lawnmower. He even listened to the croaking of a toad and the gurgling of a fountain.

It seemed that no one would ever teach him how to purr, so Pippin decided to go back home.

At home, LaterPapa and HurryMama were very worried about their kitten. He was late getting home. HurryMama stood at the window and LaterPapa sat on the edge of an armchair. For the first time in ages, neither of them moved. It was almost as if time had stopped. Maybe, just maybe, life was moving too fast for little Pippin. Their life was a merry-go-round that whirled around very quickly, but Pippin wanted to go slowly. Like all little kittens.

All of a sudden the garden gate squeaked. It was Pippin! He crept sadly into the garden. He'd never learn how to purr. He'd never be a real cat.

Mother ran out and scooped Pippin up in her arms. Father didn't move. He was still angry at Pippin for being late. But when he saw Pippin in his mother's arms he ran toward them. Father hugged them both, with a hug that was full of tenderness, kisses, and love.

Mother told Pippin how worried she had been. Father didn't say anything. He just took Pippin's paw in his own big paw. And again, time seemed to stop.

What was that sound? It sounded like snoring or like buzzing.
It wasn't Mother or Father. It wasn't an airplane, and it surely wasn't
a swarm of bees.

It was Pippin, and he was purring!

"Oh my sweet little kitten," whispered Mother.

"That's the most beautiful purring I have ever heard," sighed Father.

Pippin snuggled close to Mother. His paw was tucked safely into his
father's. Father and Mother didn't move an inch. They didn't worry,
they didn't hurry, they didn't run. They just stayed right where they
were, next to Pippin.

Pippin purred even louder.

And then he fell asleep.